An Alligator Lives in Benjamin's House

by Nancy Van Caster

illustrated by Dale Gottlieb

Philomel Books

New York

To Jennifer from Uncle Colin Wednesday August 18, 1993

Text copyright © 1990 by Nancy Van Caster.
Illustrations copyright © 1990 by Dale Gottlieb.
Published by Philomel Books, a division of
The Putnam & Grosset Group, 200 Madison Avenue, New York, NY 10016.
Published simultaneously in Canada. All rights reserved.
Printed in Hong Kong by South China Printing Co. (1988) Ltd.
Book design by Gunta Alexander
First impression

Library of Congress Cataloging-in-Publication Data
Van Caster, Nancy.
An alligator lives in Benjamin's house / by Nancy Van Caster:
illus. by Dale Gottlieb.   p.   cm.
Summary: Benjamin shares his house with a multitude of animals,
each of which resembles him and is playful in its own way.
ISBN 0-399-21489-5
[1. Animals—Fiction.   2. Imagination—Fiction.   3. Play—
Fiction.]   I. Gottlieb, Dale, 1952–   ill.   II. Title.
PZ.V2626A1   1990   [E]—dc20   89-34025   CIP   AC

To John and to our five alligators,
Angie, Jill, Todd, Brian and David

—N. V. C.

For Chris, Blake and Hill

—D. G.

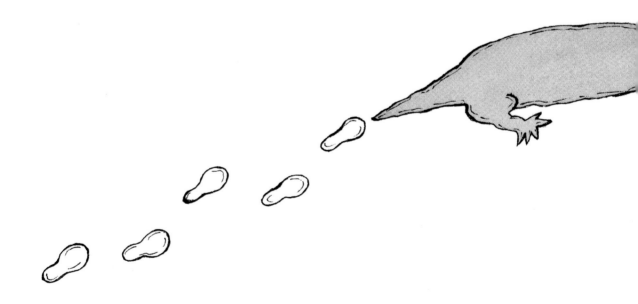

Upstairs, down the hall, under Benjamin's bed, an alligator likes to hide. He is long and flat, like an alligator, and he has bright red sneakers, like Benjamin.

When Benjamin's mom comes to vacuum the
bedroom, the alligator carefully, quietly creeps
out from under the bed and snatches at her toes.
"Grrarh!" snarls the alligator.

"Help!" calls Benjamin's mom, jumping out of
the way. "The alligator is trying to bite me. Scat,
you naughty alligator, or I'll call Benjamin and
he'll capture you and put you in a cage."

The alligator laughs and crawls back under the bed to wait for someone else's toes.

A winding, wiggly, sneaky snake lives in Benjamin's house. The snake's very favorite thing to do is to wriggle down the stairs. Sometimes he scrapes his nose on the steps, but the snake keeps sliding down.

He comes down slowly, one step at a time. And
he hisses, "*Sssssssssss, sssssssssssss.*"
   While the snake is coming down, nobody ever
goes up because they know the snake might try
to catch them.

Under the kitchen table, locked behind the chairs like a cage, a lion lives in Benjamin's house. He's a ferocious, hungry, loud lion and he has a tooth loose on top, just like Benjamin does.

He roars when he's angry and he shakes the chair legs to show how strong he is. But he never escapes from his cage.

In the living room, wearing Benjamin's
clothes, a monkey lives in Benjamin's house.

He jumps and rolls and does monkey tricks,
just like Benjamin.

Sometimes he takes puzzle pieces out of a box and throws them up so that they rain down on his head. When his mom sees him, she says, "Stop that, and be a good monkey." Then he scoops up the pieces and puts them back.

A fluffy, soft, playful kitty lives in Benjamin's house.

He has a long furry tail that only Benjamin's mom can see.

When Benjamin's mom folds the towels that
are still warm from the dryer, the kitty visits her.
He curls up and snuggles down into the towels.
Purring very softly, he lets Benjamin's mom
pet his head, while he watches her work.

A quiet, hippety-hop bunny lives in Benjamin's house. He has a bandage on his elbow, just like Benjamin does.

When Benjamin's mom is fixing a salad for
supper, the bunny hops over and sits at her feet.
"Can I have a carrot?" asks the bunny.

"Sure," says Benjamin's mom, reaching down
to give him one. "What do you say?" she asks,
waiting for the bunny to say thank you.

"Bunnies don't talk," he says and hops away.

A friendly, frisky puppy lives in Benjamin's house. He has little puppy paws that look just like Benjamin's hands. The puppy likes to run up to greet Benjamin's dad when he comes home from work.

Benjamin's dad says, "Hi there, fella," and the
puppy rubs himself against Benjamin's dad's
legs. The puppy lets Benjamin's dad scratch him
behind the ears, and then he puts his paws up
and begs to be carried.

A big, fat, slippery, wet whale lives in Benjamin's house. He has ten toes, just like Benjamin.

At bathtime he sings and splashes and squeaks his skin on the bottom of the tub. He makes waves that spill over the sides and then lies very still and lets himself float.

When his toes are all wrinkly and pruny, he gets out of the tub and drips on the floor and rubs his shiny skin with a towel.

A bear lives in Benjamin's house. It's a very big
bear. And it doesn't look like Benjamin at all.
It has a deep growl and two big round ears.

When Benjamin is ready for bed and hears the
bear coming down the hall, Benjamin jumps under
his blanket and pulls the covers over his head.

Then the bear sits on Benjamin's bed, gently
pulls the covers down, and smiles. She gives
Benjamin a kiss and tells him good night.

But before she goes, she gives Benjamin a big bear hug and squeezes him until he laughs. Then she tucks him in and turns the light out.

And when the room is dark, Benjamin and all the animals in Benjamin's house close their eyes and go to sleep.